DISNEY

# MULAN

Adapted by
## Megan Ilnitzki

Illustrated by the
## Disney Storybook Art Team

Mulan is a girl.
She lives in China.
She lives with her parents
and her grandma.

It is a big day.
Mulan will meet
the Matchmaker.

The Matchmaker will find
Mulan a husband.
Mulan puts on a dress.

Mulan makes a mess.
The Matchmaker will not help her.
She says Mulan will never
bring honor to her family.

Mulan is confused.
She wants to make
her family proud.
She also wants to be herself.

Soldiers arrive with news.
The Huns have come to China.
One man from each family
must serve in the army.

Mulan's family has
only one man.
Her father must fight
for the army.

Mulan watches her dad.
He hurt his leg
in the last war.
He can not fight again.

Mulan makes herself look
like a boy.
She rides to war
in her father's place.

Mulan meets
the other soldiers.
She meets Captain Shang.
She says her name is Ping.

Shang tests the soldiers.
They cannot
reach the arrow.

Mulan does not give up.
She climbs the pole.
She gets Shang's arrow.

The soldiers get a note.
The general needs their help.
They go to the mountains.

They find a village.
The general is not there.
His army is gone.

The Huns are waiting
for Shang's men.
They attack Mulan and the troops!

The soldiers take cover.
They fight back.
There are too many Huns!

Mulan fires a cannon
at the mountain.
The Hun leader hits Mulan
with his sword.

The cannonball hits the snow.
The snow falls.
It buries the Huns.
It buries Shang.

Mulan saves Shang
from the snow.

The soldiers pull
them to safety.

Mulan is hurt.
The soldiers find out
she is a girl.
Girls cannot fight in the army.

The penalty for lying is death.
Shang lifts his sword.
He lets Mulan go.
She saved his life.

The troops go
to the city.
They leave Mulan behind.
Mulan sees some Huns.

Mulan goes to the city.
She tells Shang
about the Huns.
He does not believe her.

The Huns come
to the city.
They grab the Emperor.
They lock the palace doors.

Mulan has an idea.

She and her friends put on dresses.

They get past the Huns' guards.

They save the Emperor.

The Hun leader traps Mulan!
He chases her onto the roof.
She pins his cloak to the roof.
She gets rid of him for good.

The Emperor thanks Mulan
for her help.
China is saved.
Mulan is a hero!

Mulan goes home.
Her family is happy to see her.
She brought them honor
by being herself.